Stories and rhymes in this book

A CHEEKY HELLO
CHEEKY CHATTY MATTIE
NEVER EVER!
BANANA FUN
BALANCING BANANAS
THE TOP OF THE JUNGLE
ONE BANANA
UNCLE CHESTNUT AND THE STRIPEY BANANAS
NIGHT DELIGHT

Published by Ladybird Books Ltd
27 Wrights Lane London W8 5TZ
A Penguin Company
3 5 7 9 10 8 6 4 2

© LADYBIRD BOOKS LTD MCMXCIX

Produced for Ladybird Books Ltd by Nicola Baxter and Amanda Hawkes
The moral rights of the autor/illustrator have been asserted
LADYBIRD and the device of a Ladybird are trademarks of Ladybird Books Ltd

Printed in Italy

The
Cheeky
Chimps

by Mandy Ross
illustrated by Tania Hurt-Newton

Ladybird

A CHEEKY HELLO

"We're Cheeky Chimps.
How do you do?"

"I'm Chatty
Mattie,
Always
chatting."

"I'm Kiki
Squeaky.
I'm VERY
cheeky."

"We're the chattering, nattering,

giggling, wriggling,

squeaky Cheeky Chimps!"

CHEEKY CHATTY MATTIE

Chatty Mattie Cheeky Chimp loved to tell jokes.

"What do you call a hippo with a grin?" Mattie asked Hattie Hippo.

"I don't know," boomed Hattie.

"A happy-potamus!" said Mattie. And she and Hattie giggled so much...

that they fell over!

"What do you call a lion with a loud voice?" Mattie asked Leo Lion.

"I don't know," said Leo.

"Rory," said Mattie,
"because he ROARS!"

And she and Leo laughed till
their tummies ached.

"I've got a joke for YOU, Mattie," said Mum.

"What do you call a chimpanzee who's always telling jokes?"

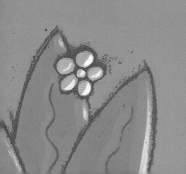

"I don't know," said Mattie.

"Well, I call her Chatty Mattie Cheeky Chimp," said Mum, "and she's FUN to have around!"

NEVER EVER!
We're cheeky,

And we're
squeaky,

But we NEVER peek
At hide-and-seekie!

BANANA FUN

All afternoon, high in the treetops...

Chatty Mattie and Kiki Squeaky practised a new trick.

At four o'clock Mattie and Kiki went to Hattie Hippo's house for tea.

They were very polite. Mattie didn't tell a single hippo joke.

Kiki didn't squeak with her mouth full.

At last, Hattie said, "Would anyone like a banana?"

"Yes, please,"
said Mattie.

"Look out!"
boomed
Hattie.
"You're going
to sit on that
banana!"

And Mattie did...

PHOOP!

Out shot the banana and... YES! Kiki caught it.

"Perfect!" they squeaked and chattered with pride.

Then everything went quiet. "Oh dear," squeaked Kiki.

"That was rather cheeky," said Hattie.

"In fact, it was fantastically cheeky! Can I join in?"

Hattie opened her huge jaws wide, and... PHOOP!

Mattie shot a banana straight in. GLUG! Hattie swallowed it whole.

Then...
PHOOP! Kiki
did the same.

"Hooray!"
squeaked
Kiki. "You
hippos can
be just as
cheeky as
chimps!"

BALANCING BANANAS

I don't suppose
You're one of those

Who can balance a banana
On the end of your nose?

THE TOP OF THE JUNGLE

One morning, Kiki Squeaky and Chatty Mattie decided to climb...

up to the top of the jungle.

It was a
long way.

After a
while, they
stopped
for a rest.

"Look!" squeaked Kiki, peeking through the trees. "I can see some lazy lions!"

"And they're snoring!" chattered Mattie.

"Wake up, you lazy lions!"
squeaked Kiki, and the lions
woke up with a start.

"Grrr!" they growled.
"Those cheeky chimps!"

Kiki and Mattie swung higher still.

"Look!" said Kiki. "I can see the hippo family having a bath!"

"Harumph!" boomed the hippos. "Those cheeky chimps!"

They'd nearly reached the top of the trees when...

"Look!" squeaked Kiki. "I can see some nice juicy mangoes!"

And she was just stretching out to pick one when...

"EEK!" shrieked Kiki! "There are two big eyes staring right at me!".

The eyes
blinked.
Then a
deep voice
said, "I can
see YOU!"
It was...

Geoffrey Giraffe. "Welcome
to the top of the jungle!"
he said... cheekily.

ONE BANANA

One banana — good!

Two bananas — better!

Three bananas — great!

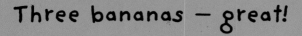

Four bananas —
go and get a...
Friend or two
or even three...

It's banana party time,
you see!

UNCLE CHESTNUT AND THE STRIPEY BANANAS

Uncle Chestnut
Chimp was
coming
to stay.

"We'll have
to be good,"
said Mattie.

"Uncle
Chestnut is
too old to be
cheeky."

"There used to be a tree near here..." said Uncle Chestnut next morning,

"that grew stripey, strawberry-flavoured bananas. Delicious!"

"Let's try to find it!" chattered Mattie.

"Yes, please!" squeaked Kiki.

So off they swung through the jungle.

They checked every
banana tree they passed...

but they could only find
plain banana-flavoured
bananas.

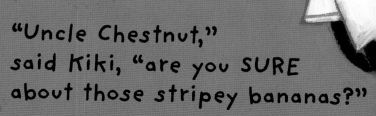

"Uncle Chestnut,"
said Kiki, "are you SURE
about those stripey bananas?"

Uncle Chestnut burst out laughing. "I was only tee-hee-heasing!" he chuckled.

"Uncle Chestnut!" giggled Kiki and Mattie. "You may be old, but you're VERY CHEEKY!"

"Quite right," said Uncle Chestnut. "But I've brought a stripey strawberry-and-banana cake, so...

let's go home and have a picnic!"

NIGHT DELIGHT

When the moon is bright
In the jungly night,

A banana tree
(I'm sure you'll agree)
Is a truly beautiful sight.